Open Minds, Loud Voices, Our Stories

By

Jalen Brooks

Mikaylah Copeland

Saniyah Daniel

Antoine Davis

Shontae Scott

ISBN: 979-8-9926537-3-1

Printed in Atlanta, GA

DFP Agency (Publishing Division)

www.dfpagency.org

Table of Contents

Foreword

Dr. Deborah Franklin (Ms. Franklin)

Entering class this semester with the task of teaching "Writers Workshop" and only having six students on the roll was daunting. Normally my classes are thirty plus. You may be saying that's a blessing to have only six students; it should be easy, but it's actually more challenging especially if they are not accustomed to being in a class this small or writing for extended times. I was pleasantly surprised to have students who were passionate about writing and had such a creative flare to their writing.

As a teacher I was excited to see these students receive the assignment and execute it with style and grace. Their creativity was off the charts. Experiencing how they could paint the picture for their readers to truly see and immerse themselves in their stories were phenomenal. To see the students blossom over the semester breathing life into their stories as you will see didn't seem like I was teaching high school students.

Many of our guest authors and editors the students had an opportunity to speak with were blown away by their talent. This group of young people have ignited my passion for teaching. These students are proof if we just give them an opportunity to shine, they will do just that. They have the talent to become the next best-selling authors.

Jalen, Mikaylah, Saniya, Antoine and Shontae teaching you this semester has been an awesome opportunity and I'm only expecting big things for your future. To the reader, you will too. These stories will inspire, entertain and keep you wanting for more.

Jalen Brooks

Dedication

To Bouldercrest, for building me into the man I am today. I'm truly grateful for all the good memories that I have acquired throughout my life. I love my Bouldercrest village, my family and friends. I hope I'll be able to share more books in the future so the next generation of Bouldercrest kids can see that if I can do it they can, too.

Poems

Yorkie

adorable/fluffy

Playing, barking, singing

I love my dog

Yorkie

Those memories fade

So distant in the far past

But so close I hope

To see you again

My dearest friend till the end

JALEN BROOKS

We dance together to remember the good times
The pain of loss always hits hard
The thought of never seeing someone you love again

It hurts but over time you start to heal
Slowly forgetting their voice
But you just try to sit and remember

Knowing they'll never be able to come back
So all you really can do is sit and hope they feel your love.

Solar City

On Planet Solar there was this very holy and peaceful colony of people with beautiful brown skin and long curly hair. We all wore different bright clothing with all kinds of vibrant colors, "We only use what our planet allows us" is the motto me and my people live by. We use solar power to keep ourselves from destroying our own home for resources, my people even created solar powered vehicles for simple transportation.

On the other side of the colony there was another, but this one was full of hate. They hated the way we lived trying to preserve our home while they just wanted to destroy it. They constantly try to steal our solar equipment so we can be forced to harvest resources and work for them our leader.

Jassius gave a speech before sending troops to get our supplies: "They will never see us as equals. They dislike our ways so we must fight for our home. They stole our supplies for their own selfishness. I know we are peaceful people, but we cannot let these monsters take our ways."

When the battle first began their numbers started to decrease quicky, and it eventually got to the point where they decided to surrender the supplies to spare their lives. Jassius went to talk to the leader of the thieves.

"This location is a place of beauty and strength our ancestors walked these lands with their peaceful ways many centuries before we were born we cannot let you stay here."

Our leader banished the thieves from our colony and they were never allowed to come close or be near our home or our resources ever again.

Don't Look Back On Love

Bouldercrest Road - a place where anything could happen. There's plenty of broken-down homes and apartments but going further down towards Eagles Runs and Paradise East it looks peaceful and calm. Bouldercrest holds a lot of memories: good, bad, tragic, and sad but there is one event from summer 2023 that sticks out the most to me.

It's a story about two mortals whose actions shook the underworld. Murdyice, the most beautiful goddess of stories with long black locs highlighted with ocean blue. Ordis, a quiet soul from the eastside of Atlanta. Ordis had a voice that could hush a crowded room; a gift for writing poems and hip hop songs that turned into melodies, and a way of seeing the world for what it actually is both chaotic and beautiful.

He was tall and slim, with long curly locs that went to the middle of his back. He always wore black with bits of white. He said it made him feel whole, like the world couldn't dull his shine. But even with all his talent, Ordis felt alone. Writing and music was the only thing that made sense to him, the only thing that kept him going.

One hot summer afternoon, Ordis was walking down Bouldercrest, staring at the cracks in the sidewalk and stepping over them like it was a game. It reminded him about the times when he was a child and all he had was his Uncle Hades. He didn't know where he was headed he just needed to move.

Then he heard it. "Aye, boy! Come here real quick!"

He looked up and saw a woman standing near the bus stop. Her hair was a bright, ocean blue, with streaks of black flowing down her shoulders like waves stirred by wind. Her skin was a rich brown and glowing in the sun, and her eyes were deep oak, almost like they held stories.

Ordis asked himself, *Who is she? I ain't ever seen her round here before. She must've moved around here not too long ago.* "Why you gotta call me a boy? You know I gotta name. Just ask what it is!"

He walked up to the woman confidently with a smirk. "What's your name?" Ordis asked, his voice shaky with surprise.

"My name Murydice. What's yours, boo?"

Ordis blinked, suddenly warm with nerves. From that moment, they were inseparable. Murydice was everything he didn't know he needed. She brought color into his dark, quiet world. When they were together songs came to him easily. His heart beat faster, and for once he wasn't writing about pain he was writing about love.

As Ordis' music spread through the city, people started to notice. The word reached someone named Hades, who was also Ordis' uncle, a sharp talking music manager with slick suits and a gold watch that never stopped ticking.

"You gon be big, boy," Hades told Ordis. "But you gotta let me take you there. No more street shows, no more free gigs, you're done struggling."

Murydice didn't trust him. "He talks like he owns you already!" she yelled angrily. "Don't let him change your voice."

But Ordis was tired of being broke. He wanted the world to hear him, so he agreed with his uncle and signed a contract.

It started off alright - studio time, interviews, a tour bus with his name and face on the side, but soon Hades had him running nonstop. Ordis barely slept. He didn't write from his heart anymore. He wrote what they told him to. His songs slowly became more and more weary and the worst part of it all? He barely saw Murydice.

"I miss you," she told him over the phone one evening. "Come home."

"Imma be home soon. You know Hades got me doing all this extra crazy mess. You know I'd rather be with you," he promised. "Soon."

But soon came too late.

One night, Murydice showed up at a rehearsal uninvited. She was tired of waiting. She wanted to talk face to face with him. Ordis was happy to see her, but Hades wasn't.

Hades pulled him aside, eyes sharp like a razor blade. "She distracting you, nephew. You trippin. Either she go or the deal off."

Ordis didn't answer. He went back to Murydice and wrapped his arms around her like he never wanted to let go. Hades watched them from across the room, his face unreadable. Later that night, when rehearsal ended, Ordis stepped out to take a call. Murydice waited near the door, humming one of his old poems softly to herself.

That's when Hades walked in.

No one knows exactly what happened. Maybe it was jealousy maybe it was rage. maybe he couldn't stand seeing Ordis love something more than fame. But the result was the same.

A gunshot.

By the time Ordis ran towards the door, Murydice was on the ground, blood staining her white shirt. Her blue hair spread around her like a broken halo.

"No, no, no," he whispered, holding her close. "Stay with me. Please."

She looked up at him one last time and said, "I just wanted you to sing for yourself again."

Her eyes closed.

Ordis didn't perform. Didn't speak. The world moved on without him. That's when Jaizer, the god of death came to him. Not in flames, not in shadows... just a man in a dark coat standing by the door of the funeral home.

"I heard your voice once," Jaizer said. "It shook the ground where I live."

Ordis didn't answer.

"I can give her back," Jaizer continued. "But only if you walk to her. And when you find her, you must leave without ever touching her or making eye contact. If you do, she's gone for good."

Without hesitation, Ordis followed.

He traveled to a place beneath the city, through quiet streets and smoky tunnels filled with memory and regret. The closer he got, the louder the voices grew. Songs he never finished, promises he broke, pain he buried. At the end of it all, he found her.

Murydice stood in a soft light, her hair glowing like

before. She smiled when she saw him.

"I knew you'd come," she said.

"I'm bringing you home," Ordis replied. "But we have to walk. And I can't touch you or make eye contact with you."

She nodded. They started moving toward the exit. Each step felt like walking through water. The voices became familiar ones. A mother's lullaby. Laughter. His own doubts.

Then he heard Hades. "You couldn't protect her," the voice said. "She died because of you. You loved your music more."

Ordis clenched his teeth. He kept walking. But doubt crept in. What if she wasn't there? What if it was just an illusion? He turned. Nothing.

The touch of her hand disappeared from his. "No!" he cried, spinning around. But she was already gone, fading back into the light.

Behind him, Hades appeared. "You were almost there," he said. "But love that looks back never leaves."

Now, Ordis walks Bouldercrest Road alone. He doesn't sing for crowds anymore. He sings for the wind, for the sky, for her. And if you walk past late enough, you might hear him, and if you're lucky, you might hear Murydice singing back.

About The Author

Jalen Brooks is a 17-year-old student that attends McNair High School. He likes to rap and write poetry. Many of his writings focus on themes of family. His inspiration stems from parts of his childhood that gives him great memories of being happy and free. He loves to joke and bring joy to his peer writers and put a smile on their face.

Mikaylah Copeland

Dedication

To my teacher, Ms. Franklin my Creative Writing teacher, I thank you for pushing me into something new and different that expanded my writing techniques. You are a true voice in advocating for young people in writing, expressing themselves in thought, feelings, and emotions.

Poems

A Crown of Light and Shadow

An image of a beautiful soul

Features of brightness mind of divine smartness

Silver is shiny but silver isn't always gold

Mind of matter achieving with greatness

Thoughts in despair of what could be

A pen and a pencil of what others may seek

All together for each other but there is no we

Continue to grow or you will be weak

Amuse to the faith of challenges

A better day set to begun

Exploring a world but is no fun

Opportunities too chase building a foundation

Time at ease focus on concentration

MIKAYLAH COPELAND

She Wears the Weight of The Day

She rotates her life

Effortlessly and quiet

The air of silence of arising trees

Her smile lights up the smoke

Stitched with pain that

Should be closed

Tip of fate is under her nose

She is life

Not a dream

Not a movie

Her soul is the rebirth

Of greatness of a wife

And though she says

Everything is fine

A mighty strong warrior

With a strong voice

And teary brown eyes

Fashion

I am decor

Colorful with creations fulfilled

Makeup in disguise

Move

Go Better

Tiring, Building, Strong

A warrior that never dies

Champion

MIKAYLAH COPELAND

The Pleasing Pie of Grandmother's Sweet Eye

In a small town in Chicago, Illinois where wind breezed amongst the trees and the air brought a sense of relief and flowers bloomed so effortlessly, everyone knew of Grandma Gail's sweet ol pie. Grandma Gail was known far and wide for many things: her heavy hands, her mouth where she teaches, and a tough love for everyone she meets. But most of all she was known for her "Sweetest Pie," a recipe passed on from great grandmother to mother and more... so many more generations.

Every year at Thanksgiving, people would call in, their mouths prepared for the pie. Waiting for Grandma Gail to mix up each batch and place it in the oven. It was made with sweet potatoes, vanilla extract, cinnamon sugar and a little bit of honey. But the pie wasn't just sweet because of the added ingredients. It was sweet because of the love she put in the pie; the soul of the body and the memories baked in the crust. Each slice held a story; laughter among family time, ancestors passing on traits so she could run and make the best out of them.

One Saturday morning as the sun set below the skies, Grandma Gail called her youngest granddaughter Milan to her side.

"Little girl," she said, her voice like a soft violin. "Do you want to know how to cook my sweet potatoes pies?"

Milan smiled wide and quickly to grab all ingredients needed as following her grandmother's recipe.

As they mixed, whipped and prepared the pies, they sang songs on her grandmother's playlist. Even the ones featuring Marvin Gaye. That night, Milan carried the pie to Thanksgiving dinner. When everyone tasted it, they closed their eyes and smiled, as if they were embracing a loved one long lost and found again.

And from that night on, whenever Milan baked Grandma Gail's Sweetest Pie, she remembered not just the recipe, but the love, the legacy, and the magic of being part of something bigger than herself.

The Relic of the Gods

In the soiled twilight of the ancient world, the air blew with a strange and unexplainable energy as the sand stays still as the wind blows within the sun. At the heart of this moment stood four strong figures, each more legendary than the last. The destinies they held were forever etched into the pages of history, but their paths had never crossed until now.

As the sun was setting over the Mediterranean, making long shadows over the hallow city of Alexandria, a hub of culture and power, Cleopatra, the last queen of Egypt, stood on the balcony of her palace, staring at the glittering waters below. Her mind was sharp as ever, plotting the next move in her ethics of politics and power. But tonight, something felt different. The winds whispered despair, and a sense of destiny hung in the air. She turned, sensing a presence behind her.

"Do you feel that?" Cleopatra's voice was soft but commanding.

From the shadows stepped Athena, goddess of

wisdom and war, her eyes gleaming with the knowledge of the ages. She had come to guide the queen, but not for the reasons Cleopatra might have imagined. Athena had a much greater purpose in mind.

"Tonight, you are not alone in your fate."

Cleopatra raised an eyebrow, confused but classy. "Who do you speak of?"

Before Athena got out her response, a figure in shiny armor appeared from the gathering twilight. His name had been murmured across the land, from Greece to Persia from the farthest reaches of India to the heart of Egypt: Alexander the Great the conqueror of the worlds.

Cleopatra's breath caught in her throat. She had heard the stories of his brilliance, of his unyielding ambition and military genius. Now, he stood before her alive in a way that seemed almost impossible.

"Athena," Alexander said, his voice rich with authority. "I have heard the whispers, too. The winds have carried me to this place, though I thought my time had passed. But there is more at stake here than we understand."

Athena nodded gravely, her gaze shifting to the horizon. "There is a force beyond time itself that has summoned you all here. Julius Caesar, too, will arrive. This is no accident, Alexander. The fabric of history is unraveling, and only you four can restore the balance."

As if on cue, a shadow crossed the ground, and a man in a Roman toga strode toward them with the confidence only a conqueror could possess. Julius Caesar, his eyes steely and focused, looked every bit like the ruler of Rome.

"I knew I would find you here," Caesar said, his voice laced with the weight of empire. "Athena, Alexander, Cleopatra together, we will forge a new destiny. What is this force that threatens the future? Tell me, and we shall overcome it."

Cleopatra stepped forward, her regal presence impossible to ignore. "Tell me this, Caesar," she said with a sly smile. "What is it that binds us all together? We are from different lands, different times. What could possibly unite us now?"

Athena's expression softened, and she looked at them all. "Each of you embodies the greatest qualities of leadership, strategy, wisdom, and power. But the world is shifting, and your destinies must align. Together, you will face a force that transcends time—one that could unmake the very future you fought to shape."

The four stood in silence, each contemplating the weight of what was being asked. Alexander's eyes burned with the fire of battle, Caesar's with the fire of conquest, Cleopatra's with the fire of diplomacy and rule, and Athena's with the fire of divine wisdom.

It was clear now: the threads of fate had woven their stories together, and it was up to them to defend the very fabric of history itself. And thus, the great gathering of legends began, as these immortal figures stood on the precipice of something greater than any of them could have imagined. The world was about to witness the coming together of the greatest minds and warriors ever to have walked the Earth.

As the relic of the gods pulsed with an ancient energy, four legendary figures found themselves drawn together across the boundaries of time. Athena, her eyes burning with divine wisdom, watched as Alexander the Great gripped the artifact tightly, feeling the weight of destiny in his hands.

Cleopatra, ever the strategist, traced the golden inscriptions along the relic's surface, deciphering secrets locked away for millennia. "This is not merely a treasure," she murmured, casting a glance at Julius Caesar, whose calculating gaze revealed his own ambitions. "This is the key to power beyond empires."

Suddenly, the relic shimmered, a gateway forming before them a corridor between past, present, and future. Athena stepped forward first, her presence commanding. "The gods do not take kindly to those who seek power without purpose."

But ambition ran deep in the veins of mortals. Alexander, emboldened by conquest, felt the artifact calling to him seeking the means to secure her legacy. And Caesar, ever the tactician, saw opportunity that could stretch his empire beyond eternity.

Yet, as their hands met the relic's surface together, the heavens trembled. The gods watched. Their fates intertwined, and history itself bent at their will. Would they unite or would their desires shatter the world as they knew it?

Only the relic knew.

The relic vibrated violently, as if sensing the collision of ambition and divinity within its presence. Before the four legendary figures could react, golden tendrils of light sprang forth, wrapping around their wrists, binding them together in an unbreakable fate.

Athena's voice thundered, her divine presence flaring. "The gods do not grant power lightly. You must prove yourselves worthy."

Alexander, ever the conqueror, gritted his teeth and

pulled against the force. "I have earned my victories through blood and strategy! No god shall decide my worth."

Cleopatra's calculating gaze flickered between her companions. "Victory is not merely in battle, but in legacy. If we wield this relic correctly, we could shape history itself."

Caesar, a master of manipulation, tilted his chin upward, considering. "And if we do not? Do we become prisoners of its will?"

The relic's energy pulsed, and the world around them shifted. No longer were they standing in ancient halls, they now found themselves on a battlefield where time itself fractured. Armies of the past and future blurred together, phantoms of war clashing in a never-ending struggle. The gods had summoned a trial.

Each legend would be tested—not by might alone, but by wisdom, ambition, and resolve. They must face their deepest fears, their greatest desires, and determine whether they were mere mortals who dared defy fate or figures destined to become something greater than history itself. Athena gave one last warning.

"Choose carefully. The relic does not grant second chances."

About the Author

Mikaylah Copeland is a spirited 17-year old from East Atlanta, Georgia. She is currently a student at Ronald E. McNair High School located in Atlanta, in the district of Dekalb County. She shines academically and has earned awards like Honor Roll and Principal's Choice.

A former ballet dancer turned cheerleader and softball player, Mikaylah loves staying active and helping others, through community service or being involved in group projects.

With dreams of becoming a cosmetologist and gynecologist, she is excited to continue her journey after high school graduation at Spelman Colleg and Atlanta Tech.

Saniya Daniel

Dedication

To my family, who have always encouraged me to dream big and believe in my voice. To my teachers, for inspiring me to push my limits and see the beauty in every word. And to my friends, who listen, laugh, and remind me why stories matter.

This is for all of you—thank you for being a part of my journey.

Poems

Eyes

Beautiful, Pretty

Looking, Blinking, Sleeping

Sadly, Desperately, Happily, Mysteriously

Glimpse Souls

Books

Studious, Energetic

Reading, Writing, Sighting

Mysterious, Joyful, Happily, Sadly

Timeless

Phone

Addictive, Distractive

Typing, Liking, Calling

Life

SANIYA DANIEL

Snow

Pretty, Cold

Playing, Rolling, Sliding

Jolly, Excited, Anxious, Eager

Enjoyable

Morning phone check sleep

Eyes open ready to kill time

Ready for my day

Stars gazing eyes open look

Trees flowing wind blowing

Beautiful nature

Beautiful nature

Hearts pumping eyes blinking

Wonderful sight

Echoes in the Scroll

The screen glows

A tiny sun in a quiet room

Casting shadows of ourselves

We can't quite recognize

Fingers swipe

Left, right, up

Seeking, searching, sifting through

Lives curated like museum exhibits

The Moon Knows

The moon hangs low tonight

A lantern for weary

A mirror for the lost

Silent witness to whispers of trees

Lovers look up

Their faces aglow in borrowed light

Dreamers follow its arc

The moon listens

A keeper of promises

And forgotten prayers

SANIYA DANIEL

The Tale of Roses

Upon the bush, a crimson bloom takes flight

It's velvet petals kissed by morning dew

A symbol bold of passions burning light

Yet laced with thorns, a warning stark and true

The rose of white, so pure and gently fair

Whispers of peace with its fragile hue

A quiet grace, like prayers upon the air

That seeks the heart where solace may renew

The yellow rose, a beacon bright and warm

Its sunny glow ignites the bonds of friends

Yet fleeting days may summon times cruel storm

And petals fall as every journey ends

Thus, roses speak in shades both bold and sweet

A fleeting beauty, life's own tale complete

Roots of the Baobab

The sun dipped low over the village of Niani, painting the sky in fierce reds and soft golds. At the foot of the ancient baobab tree, young Amara sat cross-legged, her fingers tracing the dirt, waiting for her grandmother.

Nia appeared, wrapped in a flowing indigo boubou, her silver hair wrapped high in a Gele. Her walking stick tapped rhythmically against the ground; a beat older than memory.

"Grandmama," Amara called, leaping to her feet. "Tell me the story again. The one about the baobab."

Nia chuckled, a low, rich sound. "You are a hungry one for stories, child. Like your father before you."

They sat together and Nia began, voice smooth as the river after the rains.

"In the beginning," she said, "the Creator made the baobab tree strong and wise. It was a bridge between the earth and the spirit world. Every leaf, every branch, carried the voices of our ancestors. They say if you listen carefully, you can hear them still."

Amara leaned in, eyes wide. “Can they hear us, too?”

“Of course,” Nia said, tapping the girl’s chest with a gnarled finger. “Your blood sings the same song as theirs. You are not alone.” The wind stirred, and the baobab’s massive branches seemed to shudder with life. Somewhere in the distance, a drumbeat began—steady, calling.

“Grandmama,” Amara whispered, “sometimes I dream of people with faces like mine, but they wear strange clothes. They talk of far-off lands.”

Nia’s eyes grew distant. “Those are the ones who crossed waters, stolen from our soil but never from our spirit. Their bones may rest in strange lands, but their souls are rooted here.”

“Like baobab?” Amara asked.

“Exactly, child. Like the baobab. No matter where the seeds travel, the roots remember.” Nia pulled a small carved drum from her satchel. “Come,” she said, handing it to Amara. “Let us call to them.”

Together they drummed, the rhythms rising into the twilight, blending with the song of the tree and the heartbeat of the earth. As the stars bloomed overhead, Amara closed her eyes, feeling the thrum of generations humming in her bones.

"Grandmama," she said softly, "will I tell these stories when I'm old?"

Nia smiled, a deep pride shining in her eyes. "You must, little one. You are the root, and you are the branch. Without you, the tree cannot grow."

SANIYA DANIEL

The Dream of a Nation

I'll be honest with you—I didn't think I'd end up in the middle of history. History doesn't always announce itself when it arrives. Marcus Wayne. I'm a 33-year-old schoolteacher from Detroit. Been teaching fifth grade for nearly a decade now. Folks say I've got the patience of a saint and the nerves of a jazz drummer., Maybe they're right. That morning, I showed up at the station in my best Sunday slacks, short-sleeved white button up, suspenders snug, and my brown leather shoes freshly shined. I even threw on a fedora—light gray, with a black band. Didn't matter if it was hot—I was gonna look sharp stepping into Washington.

I keep my hair low and neat, just like my old man taught me, and I've got a mustache that my students say makes me look like a detective. Maybe it does. That morning, though, I didn't feel like a detective. I felt like a regular brother with a suitcase and a quiet hope that something good might happen.

The bus was called *The Freedom Line*—paint peeling off the side, engine coughing like an old smoker—but it was ours.

As I climbed on, the bus driver squinted at me and grinned. "You look like you're headin' to church, not a march."

I tipped my hat. "Reckon it's kind of both, ain't it?"

He laughed and waved me on. I found a seat near the back, beside a woman knitting something red, white, and blue. She looked up at me. "First march?"

"First time in D.C.," I said, looking out the window. "Didn't plan on comin'. But my students kept askin' why folks are marching, and I realized I couldn't explain it unless I saw it myself."

She nodded, kept knitting. "You'll feel it when you're there. Not just hear it—feel it."

That ride was long, warm and full of stories. Some folks were laughing like they'd known each other for years. Others sat quietly, like they were carrying something heavy. We passed around sandwiches, paper fans, even a guitar. Someone sang an old freedom song, and the whole bus joined in. Even me.

When we rolled into Washington and I stepped off *The Freedom Line*, the sun hit differently. The air was thick, and people were everywhere standing, sitting, holding signs, holding hands. It wasn't just a crowd. It was a movement with a heartbeat.

And I thought back to what I told the driver. Church and a march. I was right.

The only difference was, I didn't know I was walking into history....

I followed the crowd, holding my fedora tight as the breeze kicked up. People were flooding in from every direction—brothers in suits, sisters in church dresses and wide-brimmed hats, college kids with bandanas and handwritten signs, white folks and Black folks walk side by side like they'd been doing it forever. I'd never seen anything like it.

A kid—couldn't have been more than 10—walked by holding his mother's hand. He looked up at me and said,

"Mister, are you a freedom rider?"

I smiled. "Not quite. Just a schoolteacher tryin' to learn something for himself."

He nodded like that made perfect sense and kept walking.

I wandered towards the Lincoln Memorial, the giant statue of old Abe watching all over us. I found a spot near the reflecting pool, close enough to see the steps far enough back that I could take it all in. The crowd stretched as far as the eye could see, and there was thus feeling in the air—like the hush right before a thunderstorm.

Mahalia Jackson came out first. Lord, that woman could sing. Her voice wasn't just sound—it was spirit. It rolled over us like a wave, settled deep in your chest. When she finished, the applause wasn't just loud—it was grateful. We needed her voice, needed that reminder of strength and grace.

I stood there, hat in hand, and found myself talking out loud without meaning to. "This ain't just a march," I muttered. A man next to me turned his head. "What'd you say?"

I said... this ain't just a march. It's a heartbeat. Feels like the whole country's breathin' in time with this moment."

He nodded slowly, like he understood exactly what I meant. "Brother, we don't got too many days like this. Better hold onto it."

And then, Dr. King stepped to the podium.

The crowd quieted like someone flipped a switch. You heard the whistling wind. And then,
you heard him.

"I am happy to join with you today in what will go down in history..."

His voice was steady, strong, like it had been carved out of stone. I'd heard Dr. King before, on the radio mostly, but hearing him in person? That was different.

He spoke about the Constitution, about the Emancipation Proclamation, and how we were still waiting on the promise it made.

"One hundred years later, the Negro still is not free..."

Those words hit like bricks. I felt 'em in my gut. I looked around at the faces in the crowd—some nodding, some crying, some just staring ahead like they were frozen in time.

Then came the moment I'll never forget.

Mahalia called out from behind him. "Tell 'em about the dream, Martin!"

Something changed in him. You could see it. Like a door opened in his chest and the truth just poured out.

"I have a dream...[1]"

The statement rolled through the crows like thunder.

"I have a dream that one day every valley shall be exalted..."

He was preaching now. Not reading. Not performing. Preaching. Like the words were coming through him, not from him.

"I have a dream that my four little children will one day live in a nation where they will not be judged by the color of

[1] NPR.org. (2023). Rev. Dr. Martin Luther King, Jr. "I Have A Dream." (Speech originally delivered Aug 28, 1963.) Retrieved from: https://www.npr.org/2010/01/18/122701268/i-have-a-dream-speech-in-its-entirety

their skin..."

I closed my eyes for a second. I saw my students—little James who reads better than most seventh graders, and Yolanda who draws pictures that'd make Picasso jealous. I saw their faces. And I prayed they'd live to see that dream come true.

"Free at last! Free at last! Thank God Almighty, we are free at last!"

The crowd erupted. People were crying, hugging, cheering. Some just stood still, like the words had paralyzed them with hope.

I didn't cheer right away. I just stood there, staring at the steps, trying to take in what had just happened. My heart was pounding, my hands shaking a little.

That man next to me—same one I talked to earlier—looked over. "Well schoolteacher... what you gon tell your students now?"

I smiled. "I'm gonna tell 'em I saw a man speak the truth in front of the whole world... and the world listened."

He clapped me on the back. "Then maybe they'll start listenin' too."

After that, the crowd started to move, slowly and steadily like a river. Folks were singing, linking arms, lifting signs and voices. And for the first time in a long while, I didn't feel tired or afraid or angry. I felt light. Like something inside me had been set free.

I made my way back to The Freedom Line, which was now parked in a long row of buses like a fleet of time machines waiting to carry us all back to the lives we came from. I climbed aboard and sat in the same seat. Miss Thelma was there, still knitting, a knowing smile on her face.

"Told you, you'd feel it," she said.

"You were right," I replied. "I thought I came to watch. But I didn't."

"No baby," she said, threading the needle. "You came to be part of it."

About the Author

Saniyah Daniel is an ambitious 11th grader with a passion for storytelling and self-expression. Currently attending McNair High School, she has chosen to take Writer's Workshop as one of her electives this year, eager to grow her skills and discover her unique voice as a writer.

Known among her teachers and classmates for her creativity and determination, Saniyah has always loved reading and writing. From a young age, she filled notebooks with a diary about herself, and poems. Writer's Workshop has given her the opportunity to refine her craft, experiment with different genres, and learn the art of revision and peer feedback. Saniyah especially enjoys writing personal essays, often drawing inspiration from her own life experiences and the world around her.

She believes that stories have the power to connect people, spark conversations and inspire change. Outside of writing, Saniyah is involved in the school's marching band. She dreams of one day publishing a novel and perhaps pursuing a career that combines storytelling with social impact.

Saniyah's journey in Writer's Workshop is just one chapter of her larger story—one filled with ambition, creativity, and a bright future ahead.

Antoine Davis

Dedication

To all who need to be encouraged to believe in themselves.

"Even if no one believes in you, stick out your chest and scream your defiance!"
- *Rukia Kuchiki from Bleach series*

Looking At the Stars

Getting lost in the abyss

Dreams begin to glow

If These Walls Could Talk

If these walls could talk,

They would say nothing.

Not because they don't remember

They do.

They've held the echo of slammed doors,

The hush of secrets dropped like fragile glass,

The weight of glances that never met.

They've listened

as laughter turned silent,

as silence stretched

like a layer of dust over a ceiling fan.

But they stay still,

paint peeling in places no one notices,

holding in every word never said

like breath you forget to let out.

ANTOINE DAVIS

If these walls could talk,
They would keep their promise
to keep everything inside.

Stars

Some nights I sit under the quiet sky,

And let the stars just watch me for a while.

They never ask the who, or when, or why

They only answer softly with a smile.

The wind still knows your name it calls it low,

Across the street, against the windowpane.

And though it's been some time, I think it shows

That some good things don't wash with the rain.

The flowers bloom, even when the seasons end.

They bend they break, but still they find a way.

And though the world keeps moving fast

I find you in the small things every day.

So if I seem at peace beneath the stars,

It's cause I know they're watching just like ours.

Stars of Umoja Prime

The sun hung low over Umoja Prime, the floating city shimmering with solar crystals. Zina adjusted her metallic jacket, eyeing the gathering storm beyond the energy dome.

"We can't wait much longer," said Tariq, checking the coordinates on his hoverboard. "The storm will tear the city apart if we don't repair the shield."

Omari leaned heavily on his staff, ancient tattoos glowing faintly. "The ancestors left us blueprints in the Archives," he said. "But they are encrypted. Only the old tongue can unlock them."

Zina clenched her fists. "Then teach me, Omari. I'll fix it myself if I have to."

Under the shadow of the twin moons, Zina learned the forgotten language. She and Tariq deciphered the blueprints hidden deep in the core of the city's memory banks. They sprinted to the shield generator as the first lightning bolts cracked across the sky.

Tariq plugged in the codes while Zina rerouted the ancient solar lines. The generator pulsed to life, casting a golden dome of protection over the city as the storm slammed against it.

Omari smiled with tears in his eyes. "You see, children? We are the future... because we honor the past."

The storm raged outside, but inside Umoja Prime, the people danced, their city safe and their future brighter than the stars.

Shadows of the Ninth

The voyage had been cursed from the start.

Cicero Haschwalth stood at the bow of the ship, staring at the thick mist that clung to the horizon. The waters here were too still, the sky too silent; as if the gods themselves had turned their gaze away from this place. His men whispered of ill omens, birds refusing to follow them, stars disappearing at night, the way the sea never roared, only whispered.

The Dark Continent.

That was what the Imperials in the Britannia Empire called it. The place where the Ninth Legion had vanished a decade ago, sent by Rome to explore an uncharted land beyond the great western waters. No one had returned. No messages, no survivors, just silence. And yet… in the last year, strange reports had begun to surface.

Rumors whispered through the markets of Carthage and Alexandria, of ships that drifted ashore, their crews missing but their hulls covered in unfamiliar carvings. In

Hispania, a merchant claimed to have seen a Roman soldier, clad in the armor of the Ninth, wandering the streets with silver eyes only to vanish before anyone could approach. Most dismissed the tales as madness. But Rome was built on conquest, and Rome did not accept mysteries.

Cicero had been handpicked by the Senate for this mission, leading a force of 150 men, hand-selected from the legions of Hispania and Gaul. Their orders were clear: find the truth. And, if possible, bring back what remains of the Ninth. The first weeks of the journey had been uneventful. Then the dreams started.

Cicero hadn't spoken of them to his men, but he knew he wasn't alone. He saw the dark circles under Felix's eyes, caught the way even the most hardened veterans stared uneasily at the water at night.

And then there was the voice, a whisper beneath the waves, too faint to hear clearly but too persistent to ignore. "*You should not come.*"

Cicero gritted his teeth, shaking the thought away. A soldier did not entertain madness.

"Land ahead!" came the shout from the mast.

Cicero exhaled, drawing himself to his full height. "Prepare to disembark!" he ordered. "Keep shields high, and form ranks the moment we're on land. We do not know what waits for us."

Felix appeared beside him, his expression grim. "Centurion, I don't like this."

Cicero smirked. "I would be worried if you did."

"No, I mean this place shouldn't exist."

Felix gestured toward the island emerging from the mist. It was vast, covered in thick jungles that stretched beyond sight. But more than that there was something wrong with it. The trees were grossly twisted, their branches reaching like grasping hands. The shore was black stone, smooth and unnatural, as if shaped by a force other than time and erosion.

Felix's voice lowered. "It feels watched."

Cicero gave him a steady look. "Then let us not keep our audience waiting."

As the first boats hit the shore, Cicero stepped onto the sand of the Dark Continent. Somewhere deep in the jungle, something stirred. It had been waiting.

The moment Cicero Haschwalth set foot on the black sands, he knew something was wrong.

The air was solid and thick, clinging to his skin like unseen fingers. The jungle beyond the shore stretched wide and dark, its canopy so dense that not a single breeze passed through. Even the sea, once their ever-present companion, refused to make a sound against the shore.

His men felt it, too. No shouts, no laughter, not even whispered prayers. Just the shuffle of boots and the quiet clink of armor.

Felix stood beside him, eyes narrowed. "Orders, Centurion?"

Cicero scanned the terrain. "We move inland. Stay in formation. Shields up. Do not take this land lightly."

They advanced with practiced precision, a wall of shields and steel, pushing through the undergrowth. The jungle resisted them, vines curling like veins across ancient stone, roots thick as a man's thigh rising to trip the unwary. It was not just overgrown, it was hostile.

Then they found the first sign. A Roman spear in design, half-buried in the earth.

Felix yanked it free, turning it in his hands. "Standard-issue. Ninth Legion."

The soldiers exchanged uneasy glances. If there was a spear, there should have been a body. But the jungle had swallowed everything else.

Then came the second sign. A shield, cracked in half, vines wrapped around it like serpents choking their prey. The insignia of the Ninth Legion was still visible, though faded. But the metal didn't feel right. too smooth, almost like… glass.

"Gods," one of the men muttered. "What happened here?"

Then, the third sign. The ruins.

At first, Cicero thought it was a Roman outpost, but as they moved closer, he realized the truth. The buildings were not of Roman design. The structures were too tall, the angles too sharp, the stone too smooth. It looked… grown, rather than built. And yet there were Roman markings carved into the walls.

Felix ran a hand over one. Names. Hastily scratched, as if made by men desperate to leave something behind before they vanished. Then he stopped.

At the bottom of the wall, carved deeper than the rest, were two words, engraved in the smooth stone, hurried strokes of a man who had known he was about to die: "NOT HUMAN."

The men stepped back. The silence around them thickened. Even the jungle seemed to hold its breath. Cicero's grip tightened on his sword. He had fought in many wars, seen death in its most brutal forms. But something in his gut twisted.

This was not war. This was something else, something far sinister than ever.

About the Author

Antoine Davis is a 12th-grade writer attending Ronald E. McNair High School. He has a passion for both creative nonfiction and fiction, creating stories that reflect his imagination and personal voice. Antoine draws much of his inspiration from renowned mangaka's such as Masashi Kishimoto, the creator of Naruto, and Akira Toriyama, who made Dragon Ball.

He has not yet achieved any formal publications or awards, however, Antoine remain committed to improving his craft. He views each writing opportunity as a chance to grow, and he aspires to master various genres to become a well-rounded storyteller with determination and creativity.

Shontae Scott

Dedication

This is to my family, whose love and support carried me here, especially my Momma, my biggest supporter since before birth.

And to my crazy loving siblings, thank you for always lifting my spirits.

And lastly, to me, for proving that I really could do it.

Open Minds, Loud Voices, Our Stories

Water now flows, and lively streams do run,

Bright leaves descend in dancing, swirling flight;

Through woods we roam, beneath the warming sun,

In camping's joy, we laugh into the night.

The playful wind blows cool across the glen,

Its sudden breath a shiver on our skin;

We taste adventure, do it all again,

While firelight fades and evening draws us in.

We feast beneath the stars, our bellies filled,

Night softly calls, and woodlands hum with sound;

The forest stirs, its ancient magic spilled,

Till heavy eyes find sleep on the ground.

In nature's arms, our restless spirits rest,

The wild, the stars, the fire — all were our guest.

SHONTAE SCOTT

Wind howls, trees tremble

Sun hides, yet it's morning rise

Ground pools as clouds cry.

I want to be free. To fly like a bird and sting like a bee.

The land of the free is where I exist,

but the rules in place beg me to resist.

They say I have it better than most, yet I still feel chained

because the blood flowing through my veins.

Weighed down by the red, white, and blue that I don't claim.

The laws in place that keep me from fame.

I am a star on my own flag.

I will not brag about my sins but repent in the end.

To be free is to be with He.

My lord, my savior in paradise, I shall be.

High School

Loud halls,

Dreams and pressure,

Laughing, fighting, rushing,

Finding who we're meant to be,

Crossroads.

Planet Digit

"Ugh… they never listen," she muttered, swinging her legs from the towering platform bed. The cold marble stung her bare feet until she found her slippers.

"Orenfin!" she called, her voice ringing across the vast golden chamber.

The mirror shimmered, revealing the tall steward inside its frame.

"Yes, Your Majesty?"

"I told you—lock the balcony door. Too much air traffic today."

Orenfin bowed low. "Forgive me. There was much to prepare for tonight's dinner."

She waved him off with a sigh. "Send Lahni. I must be ready."

The Queen fastened the final pin into her own hair, settling the heavy crown atop her elegant bun. Lahni smoothed the folds of her shimmering gown.

"You are the sun tonight, my Queen," Lahni said.

The Queen offered a small, tight smile. Tonight's peace dinner with the Mountain Landers was supposed to mark a new era. She had insisted on trust. She had dared to hope. For many years the digiterians had been hated and envied by the other kingdoms for their advanced smarts, inhuman strength, other worldly beauty, and deep rich ebony skin unlike any other. They were leaders and outcasts in the new world.

The great dining room sparkled with suspended lights and crystal walls. The Mountain Landers sat across from Digitia's finest— their pale faces filled with stiff, rehearsed smiles. The Queen rose, lifting her goblet. "Tonight, we drink to unity and trust."

The Mountain King stood beside her. "To peace," he echoed.

They drank. The music swelled.

Then, across the hall, she saw her father—the former king—collapse, his golden goblet clattering from his fingers.

"Father!" she cried, shoving back her chair. His breath came short and ragged; foam pooled at his lips. Others began to fall too—poisoned, gasping.

Panic burst across the hall.

Without warning, the Mountain Landers sprang up, overturning tables and drawing hidden blades. Chaos ripped through the air. Guards scrambled to protect the Queen, but the attack had been too swift.

Fury boiled inside her. She grabbed a fallen spear from the ground, the diamonds on her wrists catching the bloody light.

She moved like a tempest.

Every time she slaughtered an enemy, nothing but scattered code remained of them—their bodies fracturing into shards of lost energy, unworthy of her soil.

Her people fought beside her, blades flashing, voices roaring. They fought for their future, for the memory of their fallen king, for the brilliance of a kingdom the world envied but could never understand.

The battle raged deep into the night, the cries of the fallen echoing against the high crystal walls.

And when the sun rose that morning, it rose over Digitia still standing—stronger, fiercer, and more united than ever. The Queen stood at the center of it all, her golden crown now stained crimson, her gown torn and blood-soaked, but her spirit unbroken.

The world would remember that the Black Star queen and her kingdom would never fall, because the sun never dies.

Roses Have Thorns

I lay there in my bed with drool frosted on my cheek and the silk sheets tangled around me as I stared blankly at the ceiling.

"Ugh, why me," I groaned.

Then a soft knock at the bedroom door, followed by the clicking of heels on the squared porcelain floor.

"Oh. Are we referring to you having to wake up early for the first time ever or your engagement to Henry?"

"Hey, Mama," I sighed.

"Hello, dear. I would ask if you're ready, but I believe I already have my answer." She had one of her famous smiles on her face—it was all-knowing.

"I'm just not sure if this is what I want. I don't even know him. It's been years since we last talked, and I was taller than him with fewer teeth." With one elegant stride, she was next to me, tenderly patting my head.

I sat up, giving her my best puppy eyes.

"Can't I just not get married? Maybe I could start my

own business, or become a knight, or even go to a convent," I said, holding my hands together, pleading with my eyes. She gave me an amused look as a soft smile spread across her lips.

"I think we both know you don't have the discipline to become a nun."

"Gabby, look—I know it's hard to understand now, but when you get married, you get a lifelong partner and a friend. You get to fall in love, have your own children to love and spoil, and watch them grow into beautiful people. Some people aren't as lucky as you in marriage."

I knew she was right. I was considered lucky. I've known Henry since I was born. He was only a year older. His family was well off, and he was next in line to the dukedom. Every other girl I knew would be overjoyed. He's young, rich, powerful, and from what I remember, he was kind and a little adorable. I gave her a little nod with a quick smile.

"Um, excuse me, Marchioness, my lady, it's time to get ready. Your bath is set." Her soft, delicate voice pulled me out of my head.

"Okay, I'm getting up. Here goes nothing," I said as I climbed to my feet.

"Good girl, Gabs. This will be good for you. And good morning, Lilly."

"Good morning to you as well, Mrs. Archibald."

"I told you to call me Mariane, Lilly."

"Yes, ma'am. I'll remember that next time." She gave a bow. With that, she turned away, and the sound of her heels on the floor grew distant.

Later That Evening...

My family held a beautiful feast—going-away and engagement dinner party. Lily waited in the carriage as I gave my goodbyes. They all stood solemnly at the gate. My father's pale skin contrasted with his cheeks flushed from all the alcohol and tears.

"Come here, bunny." He placed one hand on my cheek and the other on my shoulder. "This will be good for you—and both our families. You must be excited to see him after so many years. Be well. I love you, my little rabbit."

"Yes, and remember, you are a strong and beautiful young woman. Always be who you are, because I couldn't ask for anything better. Be happy, my love." She gave me a kiss on the forehead and a comforting squeeze.

I turned to my little brother, ready to say my last goodbye. He held his head down, staring at the pavement. I was sure he was crying. Although he was taller than me, he was two years younger. He's the baby.

"Are you crying, Cass?" I teased.

"No, I am not. What reason would I have to do that?" He quickly turned his head, wiping his eyes and still not looking at me.

I turned my head, nodding. "I see. You're completely right—no reason at all. Guess I'll leave then."

Mother nudged him with her elbow.

"All right, listen—I'm not the greatest when it comes to words," he paused. "I've always been the quiet one, and you were the loud, very loud, talkative one… You'll be fine. Just stick to what you know. Be yourself. Love you." He whispered the last part, but we all heard it clearly.

"I love you all too. I'll be sure to write." I hopped in the carriage and waved goodbye to my home in Westminster.

One Week Later...

"Gabby… Gabriella." She shook me like an earthquake.

My eyes peeled open. "Yes, Lilium, I am awake," I mumbled.

"Good morning, my lady. We're about to arrive." She gave a soft, innocent smile, as if she hadn't just terrorized me out of sleep.

"Morning." I followed her eyes and peered out the carriage window. It was beautiful.

"This is the Hawthorns' castle." My mouth practically hung open. I didn't come from humble backgrounds, but I wasn't raised in a castle either.

We drove up to the gate, and there was a knock on the carriage door.

"Gab, Lil—you can come out now." Yup. He's as respectful as always. Ronan was my knight and childhood best friend, along with Lilly.

"Sir Ronan, manners, please," Lilly demanded. He scoffed.

"Hello to you too, Ronnie," I mocked. He helped us out of the carriage and gave us both a pat on the head. I think he truly believes he's our older brother.

As we strolled to the entrance, I was greeted by two forgotten but familiar faces: the Hawthorns. The Duchess stood elegantly, fair skin, long blond hair, and ocean-blue eyes. The duke's short black-grayish hair lay smoothly on his head, and his grey-blue eyes scanned me curiously. They were both adorned with excessive jewelry. Still, my eyes couldn't help but search for Henry.

"It's good to see you both, Duke, Duchess." I gave a small, polite curtsy to them both.

"Gabriella dear! It's good to see you again. You must not remember us well," she said, pulling me into a big hug.

"How could she? She was about the size of a bean last we met." They seemed nice… just smile and nod.

"You look much more ladylike now. Remember? Your hair was so big, and your complexion has gotten lighter as well." Excuse me… Nope. Just smile and nod.

"Well, come along. The help will get your luggage." I gave my friends a sympathetic glance as I walked inside with the Hawthorns.

They walked me down the long corridors, giving me a tour of the castle.

"You may be wondering where our Henry is, considering he wasn't here to welcome you." I nodded.

"Ah, yes. Henry. He'll be coming in later tonight—he went hunting with some friends, and the horse got a sprained ankle," said Duke Hawthorn.

Later That Evening...

I was now settled in my bedroom, sitting by the fireplace with Buddy, the dog I'd spent the afternoon with.

"Gabs—I mean Ms. Archibald, you have a guest," said Ronan.

I waved my hand, allowing him to enter.

"Gabriella, lovely to see you again. You look beautiful." Henry. He looked way better than when he was a boy—tall now, with that bright smile and all his teeth. Shoulder-length dirty blond hair and sparkling blue eyes.

He walked over to me, kissing my hand. We moved to the sitting area.

"So, you're older." Why am I so awkward? Nerves.

He laughed. Thank God—we're just going to ignore that.

We had a lovely conversation about the past 19 years of our lives, slowly getting to know each other again.

"It's getting late. I should head back to my room."

"Yes, of course. I'll see you tomorrow." We wished each other goodnight.

A Month Later...

I've been here for a month. It's been exhausting. I should have known from the first comment the Duchess made.

She'd been helping with my studies—training me to be

a duchess—but her "tips" quickly turned into commands. I kept smiling and nodding.

Henry liked the idea of us—but when I brought up the comments and problems, he brushed it off. "Just focus on your studies and the wedding. Everything will be fine."

The servants picked on Lily, likely out of jealousy. Either because she served the next duchess or because I was marrying Henry. The soldiers excluded Ronan for his Irish origins, just like the Duchess looked down on me because of my Italian Nigerian mother.

No talking. No playing. No helping the servants. No making my own bed.

But it's fine. It's just the rest of my life.

Then one day, walking back from the stables, I heard her voice again.

"Gabriella dear, you have a leaf in your hair," she said, her tone cold as always.

"Oh, um, yeah. I was out training with Ronan earlier…"

"You really should be more ladylike. Everyone but you know that our role as women is to be beautiful and elegant statues. Only doing when your husband says do. You'll have a baby when he wants, work when he wants, and nothing when he wants. We are flowers. Do you understand, Gabriella?"

Something inside me snapped.

"No. I don't believe I do. You want me to be a mindless puppet. A decoration. A breeder. I'm human. I have dreams, goals, and plans. I want to live. And I won't live my life for someone else."

"You can't be serious. Then what are you good for, if not to be used?"

"You must've had a pathetic life if that's what you believe. I can do anything I want. This is my life. My choice."

And with that, I turned and walked away.

Two Days Later...

I sat in the carriage, my bags packed. Lily beside me, Ronan on his horse, riding ahead. I looked back at the castle, knowing I'd never return.

Henry didn't try to stop me. He couldn't understand. But I didn't expect him to.

I wrote a letter to my parents explaining everything. I'd return home for a time, maybe travel, maybe open my own tailoring shop. Who knew? The world was big, and I was finally free to explore it.

As the wheels turned and the castle faded behind us, I smiled.

"Where to next, Miss Gabriella?" Ronan called from ahead.

"Anywhere but back," I said, and for the first time, it really felt like the story was mine.

About the Author

Shontae Scott is a junior at Ronald E. McNair High School with a passion for crafting imaginative, immersive, and emotionally resonant fantasy stories. Her writing often explores themes of self-discovery, personal growth, and transformation, offering readers vivid narratives they can deeply connect with. Shontae's stories are known for their freeing, magical spirit and richly descriptive worlds that invite readers on unforgettable journeys.

Inspired by celebrated authors like Sarah J. Maas and J.K. Rowling, she aspires to become one of the top fantasy authors in the world. Though she has not yet received formal awards, her dedication and creativity continue to set her apart.

When she's not writing, Shontae finds inspiration in rest and television, both of which spark new ideas for her storytelling. She's just a girl, dreaming boldly and chasing her passion with heart.

WRITERS
NIKE
AIR
WORKSHOP
SPRING 2025

Special Thanks

Editor

Chelsia McCoy

Your Writing Table

support@yourwritingtable.com

Book Cover

Brandon Jolly

Brandon Graphics Design

info@brangraphicd.com

Publisher

DFP Agency

info@deborahfranklinpublishing.com

www.ingramcontent.com/pod-product-compliance
Lightning Source LLC
Chambersburg PA
CBHW042030120726
47911CB00025B/446

9798992653731